JULIAN EDELMAN

FLYING high 2

WITH ASSAF SWISSA

ILLUSTRATED BY DAVID LEONARD

SUPERDIGITAL

Published by Superdigital, LLC
971 Commonwealth Avenue, Suite 32
Boston, MA 02215
www.superdigital.co

ISBN 978-0-692-97907-5

Printed in the United States of America
First Edition, 2017

Ordering Information
For wholesale orders by U.S. trade bookstores, corporations, associations and others, contact publishing@superdigital.co

Edited by Grace Soohye Moshfegh
Special Thanks: Billy Griffin

Editor's Note: No animals were harmed in the production of this book.

"For we are like olives:
only when we are crushed do
we yield what is best in us."
—Talmud

To all the Papa Squirrels.

THIS IS A T

RUE STORY.

ONE DAY EARLIER...

Jules is a squirrel who loves football.
Jules works hard all day long.
Hard work means he gets to play!

Jules' teammates join him for practice.
They run drills, study the playbook,
and prepare for the big game!

(Hard work means studying too!)

They spend time studying the opponent.
"They're big," says the Rhino.
"They're fast," says the Rabbit.
"They work hard too," says Jules.

The Owl joins them and the team quiets down.
"Huddle up," he says.

"We're playing a good team tomorrow," says the Owl.
"They are big, they are fast, and they work hard.
 It will be tough, and at times, it might feel impossible to win,

but if we prepare, play hard and believe in ourselves, we will succeed!"

Jules knows tomorrow will be hard.
All he can think about is the game.

He studies a little more.

He eats a little better.

He goes to sleep
a little earlier.

The next morning, Jules wakes up early
and heads to the field for the big game.
The team is excited and ready to play.

Suddenly, the loudspeaker blares.
"Now introducing the opponent...

the
FALCONS!"

The Zebras bring the teams together for the coin toss.

The game begins and
the falcons are tough.

The Goat is sacked!

The Rhino gets smashed!

The Fox is tackled!

Jules drops the pass!

"Oh no!" he exclaims,
"I should've caught it!"

HALFTIME

While the falcons are celebrating their lead,
Jules wonders what he could have done better.

"Didn't I work hard enough?"

"This is a tough game," says the Owl.
"You've prepared well and worked hard,
but there is still one thing you have to do."

"You have to believe."

Feeling energized, the team
charges back to the field.

"Gotta believe!"
Jules shouts.

"It's my turn," Jules exclaims.

"I gotta believe,

I gotta believe,

I gotta believe!"

The Goat throws the ball.
A falcon grazes it!
It bounces off the claw and
off the feathers and then...

Jules' catch saves the play.
The team cheers!

The Owl calls the next play. The team is ready.
"If we score here, we'll win the game," he explains.

The team sets up. Hike!
The Goat tosses the ball to the Rabbit,
Jules blocks a falcon, and the Rabbit dives…

TOUCHDOWN!

The team celebrates!

Jules hugs his friends and smiles.
"You gotta believe."

THE END